PUSH TO THE WEST

Tana Reiff

A Pacemaker® **HOPES** *And* **DREAMS** Book
GLOBE FEARON
Pearson Learning Group

Push to the West

Tana Reiff
AR B.L.: 2.8
Points: 1.0   UG

HOPES *And* DREAMS

Hungry No More
For Gold and Blood
O Little Town
Push to the West
Nobody Knows
Old Ways, New Ways
Little Italy
A Different Home
Boat People
The Magic Paper

Cover Photo: Library of Congress
Illustration: Tennessee Dixon

ISBN 0-8224-3678-7
Printed in the United States of America

9 10 11 12   08 07 06 05 04

Globe
Fearon

Pearson Learning Group

1-800-321-3106
www.pearsonlearning.com

CONTENTS

CHAPTER 1
Norway, 1870

Lars and Karin Olsen
were inside
for the long, dark winter.
The snow outside
was falling softly.
The fire inside
felt as warm
as the summer sun.
The fishing season
was over.
Now the days
were short.
And the nights
were long and cold.

Karin sat knitting.
Lars sat reading.
Every now and then,
one of them spoke.

"The book about America
says to leave
in early spring,"
said Lars.
"That way,
we will be in America
by summer.
We'll have time
to plant potatoes
the first year."

Karin looked up.
"Why do you dream so?"
she asked.

"Because America has
everything we need,"
he said.
"Rich farmland.
Nice warm weather
for growing crops.
And lots of space
to raise a family.
Many Norwegians
are going there.
Norway is crowded.

Don't you see?
If we stay here,
we will never have
much of anything.
I feel
a pull to the west.
Don't you feel it, too?
The ship ride
costs only 15 dollars now."

  Karin went back
to her knitting.
She wasn't sure
she wanted
to leave Norway.
In her heart
she had her reasons.
But she knew
that Lars
would have his way.

  The very next day
Lars began
to build a chest.
He had brought in
the wood

before the snow came.
"This chest
will carry our things
to America,"
he said.

The chest
was beautiful.
It was very big.
It was strong enough
to carry a great deal.
Lars added
a big iron lock.
He sanded
the top.
Then he painted
red and green flowers
on it.

Lars and Karin
sold most of their things.
They packed the rest
into the chest.
Karin folded
her pretty clothes.
She had made them.

She had put
little flowers
on them.

   A sleigh ride
took them
to the big ship.
And then
they were off.
Out into the open sea
they sailed
for America.

Thinking It Over

1. Do you think
   Lars and Karin
   know what they are in for?

2. What would you
   take with you
   to cross the ocean?

3. Why do you think
   Karin isn't sure
   she wants to leave?

CHAPTER **2**

Lars took a job
on board the ship.
Every morning and night
he washed the deck.
The job
paid his way.
By doing this,
there would be
money left
to buy land.

Karin tried to knit
on the ship.
But knitting
made her seasick.
She slept
much of the time.

Then one day
the ocean
was very calm.

"We're going fishing!"
Lars told Karin.

"You go ahead,"
said Karin.
"I don't feel well.
I'll just rest."

Almost everyone
on the ship
tried to catch fish.
They caught
hundreds of them.
Then they cooked
a giant-sized dinner.

"Let's eat!"
Lars called to Karin.

"You go ahead,"
said Karin.
"I still
don't feel well."

Karin knew
why she felt sick.

But she kept it
to herself.
She didn't want
to stop Lars
from having fun.
Maybe she
should have told him
before they left Norway.

While everyone ate,
Karin lay down.
Then all of a sudden
she was in great pain.
"Help!"
she shouted.
But no one heard her.
"Help me!"
she cried again.

Late that night
everyone came back
from the dinner.
Lars could see
how bad Karin looked.
She told him
what had happened.

"I was
with child,"
she said.
"But I knew
things were not right.
I'll be fine.
But we lost
the baby."

Lars cried
with her.
They slept
in each other's arms
that night.

In a few more days
the ship reached Canada.
People in small boats
rowed out
to meet the big ship.
They sold
bread and milk
to the people
on the ship.

Then the ship
moved on.

A few days later
the ship pulled in
at Boston, Massachusetts.
Lars and Karin
lifted the painted chest
onto the ground.

It was early summer
in America.
Lars and Karin
were right on time.

Thinking It Over

1. If you were Karin
   would you have told Lars
   you were having a baby?

2. What are some ways
   to save money
   when you go on a trip?

CHAPTER 3

"Can we really stay
with your aunt and uncle
in Minnesota?"
Karin asked.
"We have never met them!"

"Don't worry!"
said Lars.
"They will be happy
to see any Norwegians!
Even if we weren't family,
they would take us in.
Besides,
we won't stay long.
We'll stay
only until we find land
of our own."

From Boston,
Lars and Karin

went to Minnesota
by train and boat
and then by horse-drawn wagon.

When they got to
Besse and Per's farm,
Aunt Besse said,
"Sit down!
Rest your bodies!"

She brought out
bowls of milk.
She gave them
hot soup made of corn.
"Now tell me
all about the family
back in Norway!"

Karin and Lars
filled her in
on all the news.

Then Lars
asked Uncle Per
about land
in America.

"You'll need
about 1000 dollars
to start a farm,"
Uncle Per said.

"We don't have
that much money,"
said Lars.
"I must make
some more money.
I must find work.
I guess
we won't be able
to start our potatoes
this year!"

"You may help me
on the farm,"
said Uncle Per.
"But there is
a good lumber business
around here.
You can make
good money
cutting down trees."

"Then that is
what I'll do,"
said Lars.

Lars worked
for two years
as a lumberjack.
During that time
he heard stories
about the Far West.
People said
there were
miles and miles
of open land
out there.
"It's God's country
out west,"
they said.

Karin wanted
to have her own home.
She loved
Aunt Besse and Uncle Per.
But she had lived
with them
much too long.

And she wanted
to try having another baby.
But why did Lars
want to go
so far away?

"There is more
for us
in the Far West,"
Lars told her.

"I hear
there is nothing
out there,"
said Karin.

"There is land!"
said Lars.
He reached his hands
to the sky.
"Land, my dear!
And no trees
to clear away!
I have seen
all the trees
I want to see!"

Once again,
Karin knew
Lars would have his way.
There was no use
fighting him.
Maybe he was right.
Lars said that
land was much cheaper
out on the great plains
of the west.
Maybe this was
a good idea.
Karin began
to pack food
for the trip.

Lars made plans
with three other families.
Each family
had a covered wagon
and two oxen.
They each took along
a cow as well.

Together,
the four families

would set out
across the flat land.
Together,
they would follow the trail
that led west.
Together,
they would start
new homes,
new farms,
and maybe even
a new town.

Thinking It Over

1. Would you rather
   live near your family
   or have more land
   in another place?

2. Why can it be a good idea
   to take a long trip
   with a group?

3. What dream of yours
   would be worth working for?

CHAPTER 4

Karin knew
the trip west
would not be easy.
But she did not know
it would be
as hard as it was.

There was a trail,
to be sure.
But it was
nothing but dirt.
It was full
of holes and bumps.
From sunrise to sunset,
Karin and Lars
rocked up and down
on their wagon.

The oxen
that led the wagons
were very slow.

There were few trees
to look at.
There were
no hills at all.
There was nothing
but flat ground
for miles ahead.

Karin set her eye
on a cloud.
She watched
the cloud
as it moved along
over the empty land.
She could watch
the same cloud
for an hour.
There was nothing else
to look at.
It was almost like
being on the ship again,
out on the ocean.

Sometimes the dust
got into her eyes.

She hoped for rain
to wet down the dust.
But when it rained,
she wished
it would stop.

   She looked over
at her husband.
She wondered
why Lars
didn't seem to mind.
He kept
a sort of smile
on his face
all the time.
He talked a lot
about the great land
they would find.
He planned out loud
the place they would build.
All the while,
he looked ahead.
His eyes
were always
on the west.

Every night
the four families
stopped together.
They built
a fire.
They cooked corn soup
and ate smoked meat.
They sang
old Norwegian songs.

Karin and Lars
made good friends
with the other families.
They talked a lot
about their dreams.
But every night
Karin felt
farther away from home.
She wasn't even sure
where her home was anymore.
She hoped
that someday she would know.

Thinking It Over

1. What kinds of problems
   might you run into
   if you drove across
   the country today?

2. Have you ever wondered
   where your home really was?

CHAPTER 5

One day
the wagon train
drove into a tiny town.
It was nothing more
than a group of houses.

"You go on ahead,"
Lars told the others.
"I'll buy us
some potatoes.
I want to hear
how these people
got started here.
We'll catch up."

"How can we catch up?"
Karin asked.
"We can't make
the oxen move faster!"

"And what if you
run into wild Indians?"
asked Eric Runnar.
He was the man
in the first wagon.
"If you run into trouble,
you won't have help."

"Don't worry!"
said Lars.
"We'll catch up.
We'll meet you all
for dinner at sunset!"

The other families
went on ahead.
Lars and Karin
stayed behind.
The people in the town
told them
how to grow
potatoes and wheat
in this kind of ground.

Then they set out
on the trail again.

Late in the day
it started to rain.
Then it began
to get dark.
"We might
have to camp alone tonight,"
said Lars at last.

Just then,
they heard a cow.
It was not far away.
They followed
the sound.
The trail
had turned to mud.
But they pushed on.

They laughed
when they came upon
their friends.
The first wagon's front wheel
was deep in the mud.

"Look at this!"
laughed Lars.
"You worried about *us*.

And *you* were the ones
who got into trouble!"

"We didn't get very far,
did we?"
said Eric Runnar.
"We'll have to wait
till morning
to pull out of the mud.
It's too dark
to see what
we are doing now."

"Right you are!"
said Lars.
"Let's eat
and get a good night's sleep.
Tomorrow is another day."

Karin slept well.
Lars had been right.
They had caught up
with their friends
after all.

Thinking It Over

1. Do you worry much?
   Why or why not?

2. How do you find out
   about something
   you want to learn?

3. Do you think
   Karin should have more
   faith in Lars?

CHAPTER 6

Right along the trail
a little sign
was stuck in the ground.
"Dakota Territory,"
it read.

"We are here!"
shouted Lars.
"Now let's find us
a fine piece of land!"

Karin looked around.
The land looked like
all the miles of land
that had come before.
No trees.
No hills.
No rivers.
No people.
But she could see

the dot of a house
here and there.

The wagon train
kept on going.
It was clear
that this land
was taken.
Lars soon spotted
a small stream.
The wagons
followed it.
It would be good
to have water
on their new land.

It was days
before they came
to open land.
But at last
they did.
The stream
was wide here.

Lars was pleased.
He picked up a

little pile of earth.
It was red-brown
in color.
It held together
with grass and roots.
He rubbed the earth
between his fingers.
He smelled it.
He even tasted it.
"From this earth
our farms will grow,"
he said.

   The shine
of the warm sun
lit up his face.
Karin could see
how happy Lars looked.
She felt afraid.
She looked around
at the empty land.
She knew
it would take
years of hard work
to make this land
into a home.

But right there,
Karin decided
to believe in Lars.
His dream was too big
to hide away.
She would try
to dream with him.

That night
the group
set up their tents
on the new land.
They were tired.
They slept hard.

The next day
each family
began to stake out
80 acres of land.
They planned it
so that each farm
would sit by the stream.
The Norwegians pounded
wooden sticks
into the corners
of each farm plot.

The next step
was to fill out papers
and pay for the land.
To do that,
someone would have to go
to the land office.
Lars and Eric
set off together
for the county seat.
They took one wagon
led by two oxen.
The trip
would take four days.
They could buy
food and tools
while they were there.

The other two men
stayed back.
They couldn't leave
the women and children alone.
A pack of Indians
could come along
at any time.

Thinking It Over

1. Do you think
   the group should be afraid
   of Indians?

2. Why must people
   fill out papers
   to own land?

3. If you were Karin,
   would you be able
   to share Lars's dream?

CHAPTER **7**

"Here they come!"
shouted one of the children.
She pointed
to the wagon
heading toward the camp.
Everyone ran out
to meet Lars and Eric.

Lars was waving
the land papers
in the air.
"The land is ours!"
he called out.
"We each own
80 acres!"

He pulled
a bag of potatoes
from the wagon.
"And see
what we bought!"

he called.
He began to throw potatoes
for the children
to catch.
"There is not
a minute to waste,"
he went on.
"On the way home,
I cut potatoes
into little pieces.
We must plant potatoes
right away!"

Each family
got to work
on its own land.
Men and oxen
broke up the earth.
This was not as easy
as Lars had believed.
There was no forest
to clear.
But the grass roots
had tied the ground
into thick knots.
Even so,

Lars was happy
to be working
his own land.

Lars didn't work
the whole 80 acres
that first year.
He broke up
just enough soil
to get started.

Besides,
getting the land ready
was not the only job.
In the late afternoons,
he and Karin
built their first house.

The house
was not pretty.
It was not even
made of wood.
This house
was made of sod.
Lars and Karin
cut up

blocks of earth.
They piled them up
to make walls.
They used them
for the roof, too.
They built the house
against a bank of earth.

The sod house
was very small.
The floor
was the bare ground.
Another wall
cut up the house
into two rooms.

No matter
where Karin looked,
up or down,
there was red-brown earth.
There were
two small windows.
But the house
was still very dark.
And sometimes
a worm or snake

would fall
from the roof.
Or a little animal
would push its head
out of the floor.

In just a few weeks,
the potatoes were planted.
And the house was built.
Now it was time
to wait.
Any day now,
green shoots
would pop out
of the ground.

Lars looked
for potato shoots
every day.
And then,
one fine summer morning,
they all popped out
at once.

"Come look!"
shouted Lars.

He pulled Karin
out to the field.

She smiled.
After such a long trip,
so much had happened
already!
She felt as if
maybe this land
really was turning
into a home.

"The potatoes
are not the only thing growing,"
she told Lars.
"There is a baby
growing in me, too."

Lars was so full of joy
he could only look
to the sky.
All we need now
is a summer of rain,"
he said.
"Then you and I
will have everything."

Thinking It Over

1. What is your idea
   of having "everything"?

2. What makes you
   feel joy inside?

3. How do you feel
   about owning a home?

CHAPTER 8

There was more good news.
Eric's wife, Birthe,
had a baby
coming, too.
The whole group
looked forward
to two new babies.

For the first few months,
Karin felt
tired and sick.
It became
hard for her
to walk
down to the stream
for water.
"I wish
we had a spring
right outside the house,"
she told Lars.

"There are no springs
out here,"
said Lars.
"But we must try
to sink a well."

He knew
that finding water
might take some time.
That was why
he had waited so long
to try.
It was more important
to plant potatoes
and build a house first.
But now it was time
to sink a well.

First Lars sunk
a long pole
into the ground.
It was hard
to cut through
the roots.
But finally
he pushed the pole

about 20 feet down.
He pulled it out.
The pole was dry.

He tried
another spot.
He hoped
he could find water
close to the house.

It must have been
a lucky day.
Lars found water
on the second try.
He began digging.
A few days later
Karin had her well.

In another month
the first potatoes
were ready.

"We did it!"
shouted Lars.
He and Karin
dug potatoes together.

They piled them
into the wagon.

The very next day,
three wagons of people
came by.
They were on their way
to Oregon.
And they needed potatoes.
"We have fresh ones!"
Lars said.
And he sold the people
half of the potatoes.

Late that afternoon,
Lars and Karin
walked out to the field.
They couldn't stop looking
at their potato plants.
It was a special
time of day.
The air was
very still.
The setting sun
made the field look
like a sea of gold.

"Well, Karin,
what do you think?"
Lars asked.

Karin looked at Lars
and smiled.
"Maybe this place
isn't so bad,"
she said.

"You'll learn
to love it,"
said Lars.

"Maybe,"
Karin said.
Suddenly something
caught her eye.
"What's that?"
asked Karin.
She pointed
to a big black cloud
far off in the sky.

"Looks like
a storm,"

said Lars.
"We had better
go inside."

The cloud
moved toward them.
It moved very fast.

"Must be
a bad storm,"
said Lars.
"I've never seen
a rain cloud
move so fast."

"I'm not sure
it's a rain cloud,"
Karin said.

All of a sudden
the cloud
was over them.
It was not rain.
It was bugs—
flying bugs.
They buzzed

like bees.
But these
were not bees.
These were locusts.

The locusts
dived into the field.
"Run!"
shouted Lars.
It was hard
for Karin
to hear him.

Lars grabbed her hand.
Together,
they ran away
from the black cloud.

The locusts
ate everything in sight.
It was almost as if
the potato plants
had never been there.
In minutes,
the green leaves
were gone.

Then the locusts
flew up into the sky
and away.
They left nothing
but a few little shoots.

It was too late
to warn Eric and Birthe.
There was no stopping
the locusts.

"We can dig up
green potatoes,"
said Lars.
"And then
we can only hope
we never see locusts again."

"Our luck
ran out today,"
said Karin.
"In many ways
our life has been good.
But maybe
it was too good
to be true."

Thinking It Over

1. What are the most important
   things in your life?
   How do you decide
   what is most important?

2. Has your life
   ever made a big change
   in one day?

3. Do you believe in luck?

CHAPTER 9

The locusts flew past
Eric and Birthe's farm.
They came down again
in many other places.

Lars dug potatoes
as fast as he could.
But it was no use.
Most of them
were just too green.
They could never grow
without the green tops.
The potato crop
was as good as dead.

For the first time,
Lars became afraid.
"Winter is coming,"
he said.
"And we don't have
enough potatoes

to last till spring.
I never dreamed
about locusts!"

Before, Lars
had given Karin hope.
Now Karin tried
to give hope to Lars.

"Our neighbors
can sell us potatoes,"
she said.
"We won't go hungry.
We still have
a big bag
of cornmeal.
The cow
still gives us milk.
And next spring,
we'll plant again."

But for Lars,
the locusts
were a nightmare.
They pushed back
his plans for the farm.

He felt as if
they had wiped out
a whole year.

In the fall
the men made
another trip to town.
They brought back
more food and wood
for the winter.

The fall was pretty.
But it was short.
By October,
the snow began.

Lars and Karin
knew all about winters
in Norway.
And Minnesota
had been cold
in the winter.
But no one
had told them
how bad winter was here.
It was very, very cold.

The wind blew the snow
up against the door
of the sod house.
For days at a time
no one could go out.
No one could come in.

There wasn't much
to do inside.
Karin threw wood
into the stove.
She made little clothes
for the baby.

Lars made himself
a pair of snowshoes.
But most days
it was still too hard
to walk
to the neighbors' houses.
Lars and Karin
were alone together
almost all the time.
They could hear
the wind
whipping around

a corner of the house.
At times they thought
the wind would never stop.

"Sometimes I think
I may go crazy,"
said Lars.
"I want to plant!
Will spring never come?"

At first,
Lars drank whiskey
to keep warm.
Then he began
to drink
to get his mind
off winter.
The whiskey
became his friend.

Karin didn't like
Lars to drink so much.
"What if the baby
comes early?"
Karin asked him.
"What if you are drunk?"

But Lars
kept on drinking.

One night
they were sitting
by the stove.
Lars was drunk.
There was a knock
on the door.
It was Eric.
He had walked
all the way over
in the deep snow.
He pushed away
a wall of snow
and came inside.

"It's Birthe!"
he said.
"The baby
is coming now.
There is no way
I can get a doctor.
You must come
and help!"

Thinking It Over

1. What would you do
   if you were stuck inside
   all winter long?

2. What are some reasons
   people drink too much?

3. How do you help
   a person to have hope?

CHAPTER 10

Karin was big
with child herself.
How could she
walk in the snow
to help Birthe?

She put
some special plants
in a bag.
Lars put on
his snowshoes.
He and Eric
carried Karin.
It took two hours
to reach Birthe.

By that time Birthe
was in great pain.
"I don't think
I am strong enough!"
she screamed.

"I don't think
I'll live
to see my baby!"

"Don't talk like that,"
said Karin.
She rubbed
her special plants
on Birthe's skin.
"Now push!"
she said.

Birthe worked
as hard as she could.
Just as the sun came up
the baby was born.
"Birthe, it's a boy!"
Karin called out.
"You have a son!"

But Birthe
had passed out.
Karin rubbed the plants
on Birthe's face.
She felt her skin.
It was very cool.

"Come in here!"
Karin called to the men.
"Take the baby
and wash him.
Birthe is not well."

The baby was fine.
But Birthe had been right.
She did not live
to see her baby.

Baby Olaf
came to live
with Karin and Lars.
Lars never drank again.

Just a few weeks later,
Karin had her own baby.
It was a girl.
Everything went well.
They named her Martha.
They wanted her to have
an American name.

"Why was I so lucky?"
Karin wondered.

"Why couldn't Birthe
live to see her baby?"

"This is the way
of the world,"
said Lars.

As soon
as the weather broke,
Eric set out for Oregon.
There was no stopping him.
He asked Lars and Karin
to raise his son.
"I must move on,"
he told Lars and Karin.
"You may have my land.
I leave my son
in good hands."

"We will stay here,"
said Lars.
"It is time
to plant potatoes.
We will try again
to make a go of it."

Thinking It Over

1. What have you tried
   "to make a go" of?

2. Do you think
   that some people
   have better luck
   than others?

3. How has having a baby
   changed over the years?

CHAPTER **11**

That spring,
Lars broke ground
in a new field.
He came across
a low hill.
As he turned over the earth,
he found
some interesting things.
He found
flat stones
with pointed ends.
He found pots.
He found bones.

"It looks as if
Indians lived here once,"
he told Karin.
"What should I do?"

"I don't know,"
said Karin.

She was still
afraid of Indians.
She had heard stories.

The very next day,
she saw
a group of Indians
across the field.
They were riding
on horses.
She wondered
what they were
doing there.

The Indians
moved closer.
Now Karin
was very afraid.
She took a baby
in each arm.
She ran outside
to find Lars.

Lars stopped working.
The Indians rode
right into the field.

They seemed
to be friendly.
They spoke to Lars
with hand signs.
They told him
they did not mean
to hurt anyone.

Lars showed them
the stones and bones
in the hill.
The Indians smiled.
Lars and Karin
did not understand
their words.
But they did understand
what the Indians wanted.

"Leave these things
in the ground,"
the Indians said.
"They must stay there
until the end of time."

That night
the Olsens and the Indians

ate together.
They got along
like old friends.

A few weeks later
the new potato shoots
came up.
This year
Lars had planted
two fields,
not just one.
In the middle
of the new field
was an open spot.
Lars had saved
the Indian ground.
That part of the earth
would stay
the way he found it.

Thinking It Over

1. Do you believe stories
   about people
   before you meet them?

2. Do you believe
   some spots on earth
   are special?

3. Why do you think
   some Indians and white people
   fought and killed each other
   in those days?

CHAPTER 12

The locusts came
the next summer, too.
They hit
the same field.
They flew right over
the Indian hill.
Karin wondered
if they knew
it was special.

The summer after that,
the air
was very dry.
There was dust
all over everything.
No one ever knew
how the fire started.
In no time at all,
it danced
into the new wheat field.
There was nothing to do

but watch it fly by.
It left behind
a burned field of
black wheat.

Then there was
the wind.
One day
the wind flew in
faster than the locusts.
It blew around
in a big circle.
It blew the roof
off the new barn.

During another winter,
the Olsens
ran out of wood.
They had to tie hay
into tight sticks.
They burned
the hay stacks
for heat.

All of this trouble
did not stop

Lars and Karin Olsen.
Their minds
were made up.
"We will stay here
no matter what,"
they told each other.

One cool spring morning
a wagon train
rode in along the stream.

"Do you know
of good land
near here?"
the people asked Lars.

The people
were speaking Norwegian.
Lars was happy
to meet people
from Norway.
"We grow
big potatoes
right here,"
said Lars.
"There is open land

back behind ours.
Why don't you
put down your roots
right here?
Come inside.
Let's talk."

    Five families
crowded inside the sod house.
Karin gave them
hot milk and corn soup.

    The Olsens told them
about the locusts.
They told them
about the wind.
They told them
about the fire.

    "Yes, we have had
some hard times,"
said Lars.
"But we have
done very well,
hard times or not.
The red earth here

is very rich—
very good for growing
potatoes and wheat.
And we have
plenty of water."

    The new Norwegians
decided to stay.
They and the Olsens
never knew each other
in Norway.
But here
they felt like family.

    "This land
will be more
than a group of farms!"
said Lars.
"It will be a town.
We'll all have
wood houses soon.
We'll build a church.
And we'll start a school.
This will be
a fine place to live
for all of us."

Karin smiled.
The old Lars was back.
She had not seen him
so happy
since before the first locusts.
She felt his dream
warm her, too.

Years went by—
some good,
some not so good.
The Norwegians' farms
became a little town.
The flowered clothes
were packed away
in the old painted chest.
The territories
of the Far West
became American states.
Lars and Karin
became Lawrence and Katherine.
The Olsens from Norway
became American
like everyone else.

Thinking It Over

1. What would it be like
   to start your own town?

2. Do you believe
   that what the Olsens did
   was important?

3. What makes people
   fit in to a new life
   over time?